P9-CZV-899

A31500 299562

DISCARD

J 618.92   Singer, Marilyn
  SIN   I'm getting a
            checkup

DATE DUE			
JA2 8'10			
FE2 0'10			
JE2 4'10			
JE2 9'10			
JY9 '10			

HEYWORTH PUBLIC LIBRARY DIST

Heyworth, IL 61745

DEMCO

I'm Getting a
Checkup

I'm Getting a
Checkup

by Marilyn Singer

Illustrated by David Milgrim

Clarion Books

Houghton Mifflin Harcourt

Boston · New York

2009

Thanks to Steve Aronson, Richard Bock,
Ellen DiMassa, Dr. Brianne O'Connor,
Christy Ottaviano, my fabulous editor
Lynne Polvino, and the other great
folks at Clarion Books.   M.S.

Clarion Books
215 Park Avenue South, New York, NY 10003
Text copyright © 2009 by Marilyn Singer
Illustrations copyright © 2009 by David Milgrim

The illustrations were executed in digital oil pastel.
The text was set in 16-point Factory Light and 14.5-point Jackdaw.

All rights reserved.

For information about permission to reproduce selections from this book, write to Permissions,
Houghton Mifflin Harcourt Publishing Company, 215 Park Avenue South, New York, NY 10003.

Clarion Books is an imprint of Houghton Mifflin Harcourt Publishing Company.

www.clarionbooks.com

Printed in Singapore

Library of Congress Cataloging-in-Publication Data
Singer, Marilyn.
I'm Getting a Checkup / by Marilyn Singer ; illustrated by David Milgrim.
p. cm.
ISBN 978-0-618-99000-9
1. Children—Medical examinations—Juvenile literature. I. Milgrim, David. II. Title.
RJ50.5.S575 2009
618.92′0075—dc22   2007034977

TWP 10 9 8 7 6 5 4 3 2 1

To Dr. Beatrice Sommer,
little Marilyn's pediatrician
—M.S.

For Jacob
—D.M.

I'm at the doctor's office, waiting for a checkup.

It's time to get examined from the neck down to the neck up.

I'm feeling pretty brave, though I'm still a little scared.

But knowing what each tool is for helps me feel prepared.

First I step onto the *scale.*
Nurse, what does it say?
Tell me, just how many pounds
do I weigh today?

A doctor's scale is called a *beam scale.* You step
on the platform, and the doctor or nurse slides
the round weights (*poises*) along the bar (*beam*)
to find your exact weight.

Isn't that a **height bar** you're putting on my head?
Hey, I've grown another inch—I'll need a bigger bed!

The *height bar* on the scale measures how tall you are in feet and inches. Your doctor keeps a record of your height at each visit—until you've stopped growing.

I hop up on the **table.**
I like the way it crinkles.
The sheet is made of paper.
See, it always wrinkles.

One end of the *examination table* can usually be moved so that you can lie down or sit up. The table's paper covering rolls down to let each person always have a clean, germ-free sheet.

I doubt I have a fever, but here's how we'll make sure: The nurse has a **thermometer** to take my temperature.

People have a normal *temperature*—the heat inside their bodies—of about 98.6 degrees Fahrenheit (37 degrees Celsius). If you're sick, you may have a higher temperature, a *fever*. A *thermometer* tells whether or not your temperature is normal.

Hi! Here comes my doctor!
She says it's time to peer
down my throat, up my nose,
and then inside each ear.

Her **otoscope's** so cool—
a small light with a funnel.
We pretend she's searching
for bats down in a tunnel!

An *otoscope* has a handle and a funnel-shaped head with a light and a lens. The lens magnifies the inside of your ears (or your nose) so that your doctor can see if there are any problems, such as an infection, fluid, or a lot of earwax.

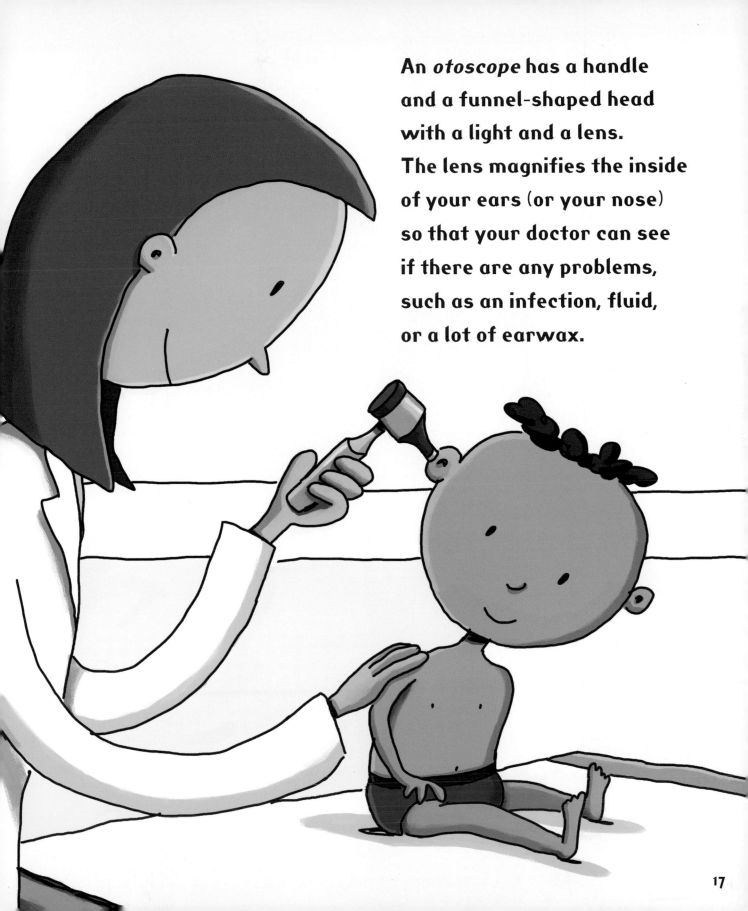

Then she takes the funnel off,
and I look at the **light,**
straight ahead, up and down,
to the left and right.

The funnel-like part of the otoscope can be removed so that your doctor can examine your eyes. She can also look down your throat, sometimes using a *tongue depressor*—a flat wooden stick—to hold down your tongue for a better view.

His **stethoscope** can be so cold!
He warms the bottom part.
Go on, listen to my lungs!
Don't forget my heart!

The doctor puts the *stethoscope*'s flat disc on your chest or back and the earpieces in his ears to hear the *lub-dub* of your heartbeat and the in-out of your breathing. The sounds tell him whether or not everything's working right.

My lungs are fine. And so's my heart.

He can hear it *thump*.

But here's another question:

How well does it pump?

She puts a band around my arm. I feel it squeeze and squeeze.
A *cuff* to read blood pressure. Don't make it tighter, please!

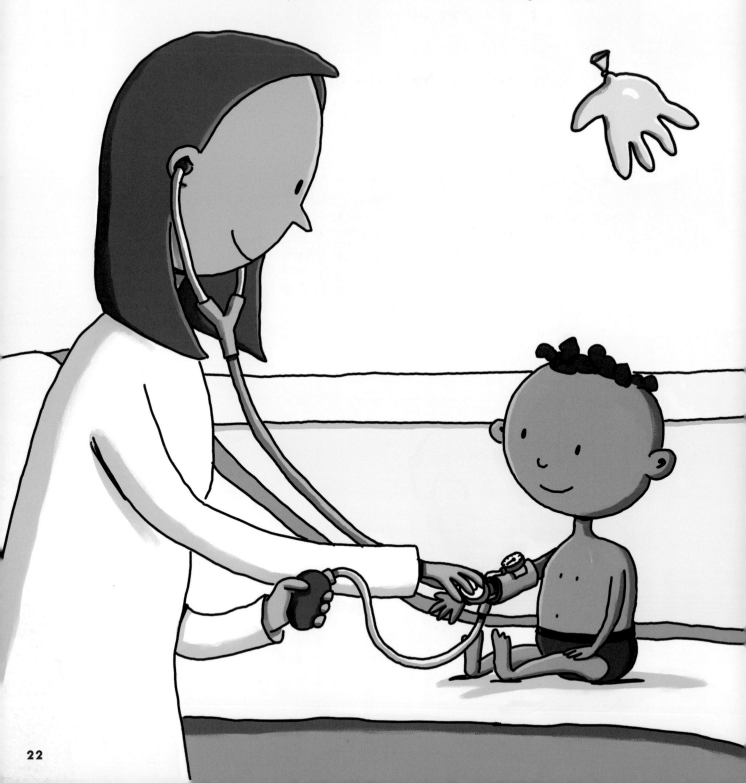

Your heart pumps blood at a certain pressure through tubes in your body called *blood vessels.* *Arteries* are blood vessels that carry blood away from the heart, and *veins* carry it to the heart. Your doctor uses a *blood pressure cuff* to check the pressure in a large artery, to see if it's too low or too high. The cuff has a really long name that's fun to say: *sphygmomanometer* (**SFIG**-mo-mah-**NOM**-eh-ter). Your doctor can also check your *pulse*—the rate at which your heart beats—by feeling an artery in your wrist.

She taps me with a **hammer.** Look at my leg jerk!
It's good to have reflexes and to find out that they work.

When your doctor gently bops your knee with a rubber *hammer,* your leg jerks up all by itself. Your nerves have automatically carried a message from your brain that told your leg what to do. This is called a *reflex.* Reflexes protect your body from things that could harm it. For example, if you touch a hot stove, a reflex makes your hand pull away. Your doctor checks your reflexes to make sure your nerves are being good messengers.

Now I've got the giggles. He's pressing on my belly.
What's it saying? Peanut butter! Don't forget the jelly!
He's checking out my organs. He's studying my glands.
I wonder how he knows so much with just a pair of **hands.**

Believe it or not, your doctor can tell a lot about you just by using his hands. For example, your doctor knows what a healthy belly is supposed to feel like.

She's taking out a **needle**—today I need a shot.

She cleans my arm. I close my eyes and think, "X marks the spot."

Syringe and injection
are long words for those things.
It doesn't matter what they're called—
that booster shot still STINGS!

Sometimes when you visit the doctor, you will need
a *shot* (*injection*). A *syringe* is a tube with a hollow
needle on the end. The syringe is filled with vaccines
to protect you against diseases, or sometimes with
medicines to treat an illness. After a few years, the first
inoculations—shots—you had lose power, so you need
an extra dose of vaccine, a *booster shot*. A shot may hurt,
but not for long.

I bite my lip. I roll my eyes. I holler loudly, "Ugh!"
"Ugh is right!" my doctor says,
and Mom gives me a hug.

I know I was a little scared—
but also very brave.
My doctor gives me stickers.
We slap five, then we wave.

"See you next time!" we both say,
and now my checkup's done.
I bet, of all her patients,
I'm my doctor's favorite one!

GETTING A CHECKUP

When you're sick, you see a doctor. But it's a good idea to visit your doctor when you're well, too. That's called going for a *physical examination* or getting a *checkup*.

At a checkup, your pediatrician (a doctor who treats kids) will make sure you're healthy and developing normally. She or he will use instruments, as well as eyes and hands, to measure and examine you, to give tests, and sometimes to give an injection. A nurse or technician may perform a few of these tests or measurements instead of the doctor. Your parent, grandparent, or guardian will be there to keep you company and to hear what the doctor has to say.

Besides checking your height, weight, temperature, blood pressure, reflexes, ears, eyes, heart, lungs, and other organs, your doctor will look at your skin, teeth, and gums. He or she may feel your spine (the bones down the middle of your back) to make sure that it's straight. Your doctor may also look at your genitals (your private parts) to be certain that you have no infection or other problems and to see if you are developing properly.

In addition, you may be asked to urinate (pee) in a cup. Your urine will be tested to make sure that your kidneys, bladder, and other organs are working well and that you have no serious diseases.

Your blood can also tell how healthy you are, so sometimes your doctor will draw blood from your arm or finger to be tested. Like an injection, a *blood test* may sting, but just for a little while.

Your doctor may also ask you to take a *vision test* by looking at an eye chart. The chart will often have the letter E in various positions and sizes. You'll be asked to say which way it's pointing. This test tells the doctor if you need eyeglasses.

Sometimes, you'll also take a *hearing test* using an *audiometer*—a machine that plays tones through earphones to determine how well you hear. When you hear the tone, you press a button or raise your hand.

Remember: If you are confused or curious, it's okay to ask questions. Answering those questions is part of your doctor's job—and it's an important part of your checkup, too.